BRIGHT STAR

Gary Crew
Anne Spudvilas

A CRANKY NELL BOOK

KM Kane/Miller Book Publishers

Brooklyn, New York & La Jolla, California

For my daughters, Rachel and Sarah,
who have chosen their own dreams. G.C.

For my mother, Doris, who allowed us the
freedom to find our own way. A.S.

First American Edition 1997 by Kane/Miller Book Publishers
Brooklyn, New York & La Jolla, California

Originally published in Australia in 1996 by
Thomas C. Lothian Pty Ltd, Port Melbourne, Victoria, Australia

Text copyright © Gary Crew 1996
Illustrations copyright © Anne Spudvilas 1996

Library of Congress Cataloging-in-Publication Data

Crew, Gary, 1947-
Bright star / Gary Crew; Anne Spudvilas, [illustrator]. -- 1st American ed.
p. cm.
"Originally published in Australia in 1996 by Thomas C. Lothian Pty Ltd,
Port Melbourne, Victoria, Australia"--Copr. p.
Summary: When she meets the famous Australian astronomer John Tebbutt,
Alicia realizes that she is no longer doomed to a life of needlework
and milking cows but that her future is as limitless as the stars.
ISBN 0-916291-75-8
[1. Dreams--Fiction. 2. Tebbutt, John, 1834-1917--Fiction. 3. Astronomers--Fiction.
4. Australia--Fiction.] I. Spudvilas, Anne, 1951- ill. II. Title.
PZ7.C867Br   1997   [E]--dc21   97-16260

Printed and bound in Singapore by Tien Wah Press Ltd.
1 2 3 4 5 6 7 8 9 10

A note on the
'Star Man'

John Tebbutt [1834–1916] was an amateur astronomer who lived in the rural town of Windsor, New South Wales, Australia. Using only a small marine telescope, Tebbutt discovered the Great Comet of 1861. Over several months, this comet grew so bright that it was visible by daylight and cast a shadow at night. Its tail stretched across one third of the sky.

In 1881, Tebbutt discovered a second comet whose nucleus was as bright as a star of the first magnitude.

In 1973, the International Astronomical Union named a lunar crater after Tebbutt and he is further celebrated on the Australian $100 note.

John Tebbutt is buried in St Matthew's Church, Windsor, designed by the convict architect, Francis Greenway. His remarkable observatories, which he built with his own hands, still stand in Windsor today.

At night, when she was alone in her room, Alicia would look up at the starry sky and dream.

She did not dream of jewels and crowns, or satin gowns, or the handsome princes who would present them to her, but of the stars themselves, and the planets, and the mystery of their movement in the deep blue space beyond.

When morning came and the nesting swallows brushed her window, Alicia would clamber from her bed, dress and hurry out to help her father with the cows. The cows were her father's life and it was Alicia's job to help him milk them.

Cows are stupid things, Alicia thought. So slow. So boring. Always with their heads low, their eyes rolling, always following one another. I would rather be a swallow, free to come and go.

But Alicia had little time to think of such things. She had other jobs to do. There were chickens to feed and eggs to be gathered and breakfasts to be served to her brothers, who set off for the fields or the orchard or the market or even the tavern, if they chose, without so much as a thank you or a nod in her direction.

My brothers are like swallows,
she thought, coming and
going as they please.

When she had finished her chores and delivered the milk, Alicia went to school, where she was happier.

Every subject was a joy to her, especially mathematics, at which she was very bright. Mr Hagley, her teacher, told her that she was a pleasure to teach. Never did she receive such praise at home.

But on Wednesdays, Alicia would gladly have missed school altogether.

On Wednesdays, after lunch, Alicia's class was divided. The girls were sent to practice needlepoint and china painting with sour Miss Simpson, while the boys trooped off laughing with Old Joe to learn nature study and fly-fishing and bushcraft, and sometimes they wandered so far that it was night before they found their way home.

'Please Mr Hagley,' Alicia begged, 'can't I go with the boys? Just once?'

'Boys will be boys,' he answered, and Alicia lowered her eyes and followed the girls as she was told. Like a cow, she thought. Like one of our cows.

Then one Wednesday, something set Alicia dreaming as she had never dreamed before.

'This afternoon,' announced Mr Hagley, 'instead of our usual activities with Miss Simpson and Old Joe, we are having a visitor. Mr Tebbutt, the astronomer, is coming to speak to us about his observations of the heavens.'

Alicia was amazed. The famous Mr Tebbutt was coming to talk to children? Though he lived on the hill not a mile from her house, Alicia had never thought to meet him. If she passed him in the lane or saw him in the town, she did not greet him as a neighbor. He was too important for that. Alicia had seen a photograph of him in a newspaper clipping sent all the way from London. Her mother kept it in the family Bible. 'The Star Man', it called him. 'Discoverer of the comet of the century.'

'Will he answer questions?' Alicia asked.

'Provided that you leave some for the others,' Mr Hagley replied, though the boys were already fidgeting.

So the Star Man came. He brought charts of the heavens and models of the planets and the telescope with which he had first sighted his comet, when it was no more than a glimmer in the western sky. And when he was done with talking, he picked up a piece of chalk — just ordinary chalk that Mr Hagley used and the boys stole to throw at one another — and turned to the blackboard. He drew a circle, which was the sun, and a smaller circle, which was the earth, and then a great arc which swept about both. 'What might this be?' he asked.

Alicia's hand shot up. 'Geometry,' she answered.

The Star Man smiled. 'Indeed it is. The geometry of space. And can you tell me what shape I have drawn?'

'An ellipse.'

'And why have I drawn an ellipse?'

'Because that is the path of a comet as it rotates about the sun and the earth.'

Then the Star Man moved closer to Alicia's desk and knelt down beside her. 'You are a bright child,' he said. 'You will go far.'

But that night at dinner, when Alicia told her father what had happened, he did not seem to hear.

On the Sunday following his visit, Alicia saw the Star Man in church. He sat alone in his pew, looking out through the window.

He is watching the swallows, Alicia thought. He has
forgotten me.

But she was wrong.

When the service was over, and Alicia stood with her family in the yard, the Star Man passed them by — as he always did — then stopped and turned back.

'Your daughter is very bright,' he said to her parents. 'I have an observatory, you know, at my house on the hill. It would be good if you could bring her there.'

Alicia's father said nothing.

The next evening, when her father and brothers were asleep, Alicia's mother came to her and said, 'There is apple pie left over from dinner. We could take it to the Star Man if you like.'

'Could I see his observatory?' Alicia asked. 'Inside it, do you think?'

'Put on your boots and scarf,' her mother said. 'I will fetch the lamp.'

The Star Man was delighted with the pie and accepted it willingly. 'You have arrived at a perfect time,' he said. 'I have adjusted my telescope for the evening's viewing. You are very welcome, if you would care to stay,' and he opened the door wider for them to enter.

Never had Alicia seen such a room. At its center a mighty telescope angled upward to the open sky.

'Come, take a look,' the Star Man said and he led Alicia to the telescope and offered her his seat. 'Tell me,' he asked when she was settled, 'what do you see?'

'The moon,' Alicia whispered. 'The craters on the surface of the moon…'

'And now?'

'The stars. A galaxy of stars…'

'And now?'

Far away, in deepest space, a shining comet lit the sky and from its tail sprang other tails, smaller, but just as bright and equally beautiful.

'Is that your comet?' Alicia wondered aloud.

The Star Man shook his head. 'My comet has come and gone,' he answered.

'But it will come back, won't it?'

The Star Man smiled. 'Comets are not like swallows, free to come and go as they choose. They are governed by rules, by the geometry of space. That is a subject we know little about.'

'What will become of it, where will it go?'

'It will glide on through the heavens, exploring star after star, planet after planet, sun after unknown sun. That's what will become of it.'

'And will it ever return?'
    'Yes, one day, in a thousand million years, it will light our sky again.'

'We should go,' said Alicia's mother, reaching for the lamp. 'We must be up early to milk the cows.'

Alicia followed as she was told, then stopped. 'May I come back?' she asked, turning at the door.

'That is a question I cannot answer,' said the Star Man. 'It is a choice only you can make.'

Ａnd in the morning, when the lowing cows woke her from her dreaming, Alicia knew that he was right.